TEN
DIRTY
DEMANDS

paige press

TEN
DIRTY
DEMANDS

NEW YORK TIMES BESTSELLING AUTHOR
LAURELIN PAIGE

Paige Press
Leander, TX 78641

Ebook:
ISBN: 978-1-957647-34-0

Paperback:
ISBN: 978-1-957647-35-7

Editing: Erica Russikoff
Proofing: Michele Ficht
Cover: Laurelin Paige

Man in Charge

Man in Love

Man for Me (a spinoff novella)

First and Last

First Touch | Last Kiss

Hollywood Standalones

One More Time

Close

Sex Symbol

Star Struck

Dating Season

Spring Fling | Summer Rebound | Fall Hard

Winter Bloom | Spring Fever | Summer Lovin

Also written with Kayti McGee under the name Laurelin McGee

Miss Match | Love Struck | MisTaken | Holiday for Hire

Written with Sierra Simone

Porn Star | Hot Cop

ONE

"NOT HAPPENING," I say, adamant despite Sabrina's pleading expression. I don't know which is harder to look at—her puppy dog eyes or the red and white monstrosity on the hanger she's holding.

She takes a step toward me. "But Donovan..."

I don't let that *but Donovan* go anywhere. "Not a fucking chance." I scoot past her to adjust my bow tie in the bedroom mirror. Or to pretend to adjust it so that I don't have to look at her, which backfires because, well, mirror's happen to be reflective, and I can still see the pout of her mouth and the tension in her chest as she holds her breath, praying I'll change my mind.

Knowing I'll change my mind.

Because don't I always when it comes to her?

"Fuck," I mutter under my breath.

She obviously hears me since her smile is hopeful when I turn around. I glance at her lips and then again at the suit. The thing has to weigh a ton. Wearing it over my tux, I'm sure to get heat stroke, and no way am I putting that rented piece of shit against my bare skin. I shudder to think about who else has sweated into the fabric.

No. It's too awful. "Nate would be a better option for this." I have no qualms about offering up my business partner for the job. He'd do the same for me. "Or anyone else at the office. Stan. Or that new guy in sales."

She's shaking her head before I even finish talking. "This party is a gift for the staff. We're not asking anyone to do anything. This is their night off. And Nate...well, I already asked, and he said you'd already bribed him to show up so no."

Of course he'd say no, not just because he has other things he'd rather do with a Saturday night. He has self-respect and isn't wrapped around Sabrina's little finger. Not for the first time, I lament that our other partner Weston is in France, running the Reach office there.

He'd have done it. I might have had to twist his arm, but that would have been easy enough.

If I do this, he'll find out. Across the ocean or not, he'll find out and he'll never let me live it down.

He's my best friend, but I hate giving the asshole the satisfaction. "We don't have to have a Santa," I insist. "It's not like there are kids at the company party. No one is going to miss him."

"*I'll* miss him."

And that's why I'll do it. That's why I'll put on this fucking outfit and sweat like a pig, because this year she took over the Reach holiday party for the first time, and if it doesn't go as she planned—if there's no stupid Santa giving out the holiday bonus checks because the man who'd been hired got the goddammed flu at his mall gig earlier in the day—then she'll consider the whole event a failure.

She'll consider *herself* a failure, and as the man who loves her more than life itself, I cannot allow that thought to even cross her mind.

Which is why I'm about to consent to playing Santa myself.

Kill me now.

"Fuuuucck," I say again, drawing it out on a sigh. "Will it even fit? The thing looks pretty large."

Excited now that she knows I'm about to relent, she throws the horrible thing at me so she can pick up some round puffy thing from the bed. "You wear this to fill it out," she says. "Makes you jolly."

"Honey, it's going to take a whole lot more than a pillow strapped around my waist to make *me* jolly." I take it from her, though, and inspect it before tossing it back to the bed. I'd rather be dressed baggy than wear the stifling padding.

I transfer the suit to my other arm as she steps toward me to run her hand over my chest. "I was hoping my outfit would be what made you jolly."

God, she's good. The seductive tone in her voice, the flutter of her eyelashes, and yes, the super short Santa's helper costume she's donned is much appreciated. It's red and fake-fur lined, and the cleavage she's sporting has me imagine ways I could add a bit of white to her look. "I'd be jollier if I could skip this whole party and spend the evening getting you out of that outfit instead."

"Think of that as your reward after the party is over."

"You can't offer what's already mine as a reward." I slip my hand under her dress, and to remind her just who belongs to who, I squeeze her ass. Too bad she's wearing panties.

"I'll owe you one," she says, suddenly serious. I can feel her awareness of the ticking clock. I'm well aware of the time. We don't have all night to negotiate, but we don't have to rush quite yet.

"Oh, you'll owe me more than one." I release her so I can examine the suit. The beard is attached to the hat —clever—but it's scratchy as hell.

"How much will it take?" She crosses her arms over her chest, and I wonder if she realizes that the gesture makes her breasts even more pronounced, if that's a tool she's wielding purposefully or if it's entirely coincidental.

Honestly, she could just stand like that for another few minutes and let me have my naughty thoughts, and I'd be...

Well, I'm not going to be happy. Not playing fucking Santa Claus, but I'm not exactly not happy. It's hard to be discontent with my life at all when she's in it.

Not telling her that though. Especially when I see an opportunity to salvage this night another way. "Ten."

"Ten favors? I owe you *ten* favors for this one?"

"Yep. And I decide the favors."

"So ten demands, you mean." She knows me so well.

"Ten *dirty* demands."

"Fine." She scowls, but I know how much she likes this kind of play. Her pretending that she doesn't is part of the kink.

"Okay, then. Give me your panties, and we'll seal this deal."

She doesn't jump up and down, but she's as giddy as she gets as she scrambles to get her panties off over her heels. She bunches them into a ball, as though they're something she wants to keep secret, and passes them over. She gives me a peck on the lips. "That's one," she says.

I want the kiss to go longer and deeper, but she's already started the countdown, and this isn't where I want to spend my demands.

Before I can deliver another one, however, she's poking me with her finger. "Get dressed, Santa."

"No fucking way am I going outside in this get-up. I'll change when we get there."

She twists my wrist so she can look at my watch. "Then we better leave now."

We'll be plenty early, even if we delay departure for another fifteen minutes, but just then, my cell rings with the tone that indicates the limo's waiting downstairs, and now that I think about it, what I have in mind can easily be taken care of on the ride over

I stuff her panties into the inside pocket of my tux. "Lead the way, my love." And lucky me, I don't even have to demand the show she gives when she bends down to put on her heels on the way out. She gives it to me absolutely free.

TWO

WE'VE ONLY JUST PULLED AWAY from the curb when I make my next demand. "Play with yourself. Get yourself wet."

She glances toward the front of the car. The glass is closed between us and the driver, but it's clear, which I'm guessing is the reason that she keeps her legs closed and her skirt covering her hand as she slides it underneath. "Three," she says, counting off this task like there's an invisible checklist.

"No, no, no. I need to see."

I try to pull up her skirt, but she shoos my hand away. "That will cost you another demand."

"Like hell it will. How do I even know what you're touching? You could be rubbing the top of your thigh for all I know. I need your legs spread and your cunt glistening for it to count."

She hesitates, her eyes flicking again toward the glass. When I don't offer to close the current, she moves to the seat facing me, which I wholeheartedly approve of, because then she pulls up the tiny skirt and spreads her thighs apart and the view is better than what's out our window, Rockefeller Center, all lit up with Christmas.

I remain stoic, but my eyes are transfixed as she draws her finger up and down her seam before nestling it inside her folds where her clit is buried. "I still say it counts as two demands."

I know her better than I know myself, and there's no doubt in my mind the argument isn't genuine. She likes the fight, just as much as she likes the submission. Just as much as she likes the fact that she's baring her pussy to me while another man sits in the front seat unaware.

"Don't try to reduce your sentence, Sabrina. The demand is that you play with yourself for my entertainment, and that means doing whatever you need to make sure I'm entertained."

"I could do the job with sound alone." She's already breathless, and she's right—the little moan that passes her lips as she speeds up the swirl of her finger against her clit is quite entertaining.

Despite her words, she brings one heel up to the seat next to her ass, tilting her pelvis backward, giving me an even better view, and fuck she's wet. Not only can I see it, but I can hear how slick she is as she draws the moisture from her entrance to her clit, and it's all I can do not to lean forward and draw that swollen little bud into my mouth and make a feast of her.

But we're only a block away from Reach, and her rhythmic whimper and inability to keep her eyes open says she's close to coming, and that means it's time to..." Stop," I say.

"Stop?" Her hand doesn't rest. "But I'm almost there."

I lean forward and grab her hand before she explodes. "I know," I say when she opens her eyes to give me a questioning glare. "That's why I said stop."

This time, her scowl is authentic as she understands what I'm up to. "You asshole."

"You love it."

She drops her foot from the seat with a stomp and throws her skirt down to cover herself, much like a little girl having a tantrum. "Don't be so sure of yourself," she huffs.

"So frustrated. And so entitled. It's almost as though you forgot these demands are supposed to be about satiating me, not you."

"Like I said—asshole." I'm still holding her hand, and when she tries to pull it away, I clutch tighter.

She responds by yanking with more force, so I move over to her side of the car so I can keep hold of her hand and put my other arm around her while I continue to patronize her. "You didn't think I'd make this easy, did you?"

The car starts to slow and pull toward the curb, and she seems to recognize the futility of wrestling with me further when we don't have the opportunity to let it turn into anything fun. "That definitely counts as number three," she says. "The show was one, the stopping was another."

I'll give that to her, though I don't admit it out loud. Instead, I bring her still wet fingers up to my nose and sniff. Her eyes are dark as they widen, and a shudder runs through her.

But then the driver opens the door on her side, and when she jerks her hand back, this time I let it drop.

She climbs out, managing to keep her skirt down as she does—believe me, I look. As for myself, there's no hiding how aroused I am. Perhaps I should be grateful that I have the Santa suit to carry as I step out of the car.

No, that's going too far.

But she's wet and aroused and without panties, and knowing this evening will be difficult for both of us sure makes it a whole lot less dreadful.

THREE

TWO AND A HALF HOURS LATER, the party is in full swing, and while the Santa suit is just as hot and stifling as I'd imagined, I'm surprised to find that intermingling with my employees in the get-up isn't all that terrible. There are even some unexpected benefits. It reduces the need for small talk—I fucking hate small talk—and I'm able to throw around the word "Ho" without having to be worried about a lawsuit.

The downside, however, is that, as Sabrina had expected, everyone loves the idea of Santa for Grownups, which has meant I've been surrounded all night long. The event photographer has basically been glued to my side, and while Sabrina has been as well, there hasn't been much opportunity to demand anything dirty.

Finally, all the bonus checks have been distributed from my bag of gifts, and most of my employees are either huddled around tables with their favorite coworkers or making a spectacle of themselves on the dance floor. Someone has opened a door to the balcony, so a cool breeze sweeps through the ballroom just as Sabrina puts a tumbler of scotch in my hand.

"I'm very happy right now," she says before she takes a sip of her champagne, and I have a feeling the source of her mood is not the alcohol. The party's a success, and she's thrilled, and she credits a good deal of that to her husband dressing up as Kris Kringle, which is fucking bullshit. The event is a success because of *her* and her alone. I could tell her, I *should* tell her, but I actually am an asshole when it comes to expressing how I feel with words. I'm much better with action, and that means it's time for another one of my demands.

Because, despite what I said earlier, the demands are about her, not me. Just like everything I do is about her. My greatest, and perhaps only, gift is being able to know exactly what she needs, and right now I know she needs a reward.

I get the chance to give her one when her assistant

approaches us. "I got my gift earlier, but I need a photo with Santa," Roxie says. "Weston will never believe you did this without proof."

Of course it would be Roxie who betrays me. She was Weston's assistant for the first five years the company was in business. Sabrina inherited her when he moved to France, and she took over his job.

"You traitor," I (mostly) tease. "If it had to be anyone, I'm glad it's you, I suppose. Hop on." Praying that my Human Resources director isn't watching, I spread my legs wide so she can perch on my knee without being too inappropriate. Then, I look at Sabrina. "Santa's helper should get in on this too, don't you think, Roxie?"

"Oh, yes! The more the merrier."

Sabrina takes my drink from me and sets it down nearbly along with hers before settling herself on my lap. Wrapping an arm around her, I scoot her back so that her ass hangs a little over my thigh, giving me access to what's underneath her skirt. Her breath hitches when she feels the first stroke of my finger around the rim of her cunt.

"Stay still. Don't make a sound," I whisper-demand in her ear.

"That's four," she whispers back.

"I said don't make a sound." I pinch her sensitive skin in reprimand, and good girl that she is, her lips part, but she's silent.

Of course I have to torture her. The tip of my finger slides easily inside her. Has she been wet all night in anticipation of whatever I'd make her do next?

My dick jumps at the thought, and when the photographer prompts us all to say, "Be Merry!" instead of the traditional "Cheese", it's a real smile I deliver.

She shivers, but she manages to suppress sound, even when I insist on several more shots, "Just to be sure we got a good one," before agreeing with Roxie that we probably did.

Sabrina—and my finger—are soaked when I allow her to stand. "Well played," she says.

"Well taken," I say in return, despite the fact that she bobbles when she tries to take a step.

I stand up, but I'm not quick enough to catch her. Fortunately, Nate is. "Whoa there. You okay, Sabrina?"

"Got up too fast," she lies. Her blush would only give her away to someone who's good at spotting dirty goings-on.

As it happens, Nate is particularly talented in that area.

It's not him, however, that calls her out. "I've used

that excuse a time or two myself," Trish says with a wink.

Sabrina's blush deepens, and I have to bite back a smirk before I greet my partner and his...well, his Trish.

The two aren't married. They don't even like the term "partners", but they're together. She claims she'll never live with anyone, but Nate bought the place right next to her, and last I'd heard, they were breaking down a wall to connect the two.

He's head over heels for her, and she's as devoted to him as she'll ever be to anyone. Of course, they're also regular members at the city's most elite sex club, and more than once, Nate has invited me and Sabrina into their bed.

To which I've said no thank you.

No shame on open relationships, but I'm not keen on sharing, and I don't believe anyone else can give Sabrina what she needs like I can. If I did, if she wanted something more, then I'd have to revisit my reservations. Thankfully, I don't foresee it as an issue.

Meantime, I don't see any harm in using their sexual proclivities to our advantage. After looking to be sure no one else is in earshot, I pull out my next demand. "Sabrina, why don't you tell our friends just what you're blushing about?"

She throws me a look of outrage that suggests that maybe she isn't quite as on board with sharing her shame as I thought she would be.

Nate reads it as such, anyway. "She doesn't have to—"

"Actually," I interrupt. "She does. If I demand it."

"Ah, it's that kind of game." Nate pulls Trish into his side. "We were playing a game like that earlier, weren't we, Trish?"

She nods. "Except in our version of the game, I got to be Santa. If Santa is synonymous with Sir."

"How else do you think she got me in this suit?" I'm staring right at Sabrina, looking for any cues that tell me I'm pushing her too far, divulging too much. Her breathing has picked up. Her pupils have darkened. She swallows. Yes, she's into this. Timid about it, perhaps, but into it.

"Trish makes a wicked Domme. If you need any ideas," Nate offers.

But I don't need ideas, and the panicked flit of Sabrina's eyes says that's out of her comfort zone. "We're good, thanks. Or we will be good as soon as Sabrina tells you what we were doing. Unless you'd rather we show them?" I address the last part to her. It's an empty threat, but one meant to push her into action, and it does the job.

"Santa did bad things to me while I was sitting on his lap." She keeps her gaze locked on mine.

"Oh, I love stories that start with bad things and laps." Trish waggles her brows. "Tell me more."

Knowing Sabrina won't be specific if I don't prod her, I add, "Be specific."

She narrows her eyes, and I feel that adrenaline rush that accompanies so much of our sex—the thrill of pushing her to her limits of humiliation or degradation. The joy from knowing that she'll go there with me. Of knowing that I'm the one she trusts to take her there.

Bravely, she tells them. "He put his finger inside me while the photographer took pictures."

Put that way, it sounds even dirtier than it was.

I don't bother to clarify. "Inside you...where? Use your words, Sabrina. Even if they're naughty."

"Especially if they're naughty," Nate agrees, then seems to reconsider. "Is this considered creating a toxic work environment?"

"Yes. Definitely. I'll give her all my shares if she decides to divorce me because of it."

She doesn't seem to have a problem with it, though, since she responds with, "Donovan slipped his hand under my skirt, put his finger in my pussy, and told me not to make a sound."

"And did she?" Trish seems genuinely interested in the answer.

"Not a peep," I say, proudly.

She flashes her hand at me, fingers spread, and it takes a second before I realize she's telling me that was my fifth demand.

"You're about to get number six," I say quietly so that only she can hear as I pull her to my side and rest my hand on her hip. I love how it makes me feel like she's mine, and of course she is mine, but there's a part of me that is still surprised everyday that I wake up with her next to me. I'll never tire of claiming her with these small gestures. "I believe I promised you something that would make this night worth your while, Nate."

"That you did. Is it hiding in there?" Nate nods to the now empty Santa bag at the side of my abandoned chair.

"Worth too much to leave it there. Sabrina, would you mind going out to the coat check and get the box of Cubans I stowed in there earlier?" She turns toward me, her brow wrinkled at the request, having expected a demand, not realizing it's still to come until I dip my mouth to her ear and whisper. "Grab three, but before you come back, put one of them—the one that you intend to give to me—inside your pussy first. I want to be able to taste you when I light it up."

She gives me a half-scandalized, half-exhilarated look, and I'm half-expecting she'll push back, but she surprises me and just says, "Okay."

Then, with her body angled so that no one can see, she puts her hand directly on my already half-stiff cock —not an easy feat to find under the baggy suit—and squeezes before going on her way.

God, she's filthy. How the hell did I get so lucky?

My mind is already ten steps ahead of where she is physically. Twenty. Imagining her slip into the coatroom, her apology to the attendant who lets her in because of her credentials, Sabrina's furtive glances toward him as she waits until he's distracted before taking a thick cigar out of the box and slipping it quickly inside her. Imagining how much the entire scenario turns her on.

"She's coming along," Nate says, pulling me from the fantasy.

I bristle at his words. *Coming along.*

As though she's an animal who needs training.

As though she's playing tonight simply for my benefit.

As though she's not already exactly who she should be.

I level a stern stare at my partner. "The game is for her," I say, even though I don't owe him any explanation, and I certainly don't expect him to understand. For him, love is about both partners exercising their passions together.

For me, it's about Sabrina.

"You're good at giving her what she wants." I suspect Trish says it in an attempt to smooth my feathers.

I don't need validation, but I'm not the type to play humble. "I try," I say in a tone that says *I know*.

"How good is she at giving you what you want?" Nate asks, and the way he seamlessly picks up where his...Trish...left off, I almost feel ganged up on.

I pivot my whole body when I turn toward him this time. "What are you suggesting, Nate? That there's something lacking in our relationship? There's not."

He raises his hands in surrender. "That's not what I'm saying at all. You can back down."

Telling me to back down is the best way to get me to do the exact opposite, but because of the occasion—

because Nate is my friend, and I know he means no harm—I convince myself to take a breath before I respond. "What, then, are you saying? I'm interested."

"I'm saying that you give all you are to making sure her every passion is met. You look after her in every way possible—look after all the people you care about, for that matter. It's admirable how much you sacrifice for us, leading us all to what we want most. I'm just curious if she takes care of you? If you'd let her."

It's a fair enough question, though the point is moot. The thing I want most, the thing I care about most—it's her. Keeping her is all I need.

"She would take care of me," I assure him. "If I—"

"Needed taking care of," he finishes for me, correctly predicting my thought. "Got it." He manages not to roll his eyes, but I can still hear the hint of it in his tone. He's the type who believes everyone needs taking care of. He's not wrong about that.

He's just wrong to include me with *everyone*.

Sabrina returns with a clipped pace that I am certain is attributed to excitement. "Delivery on Santa's behest!" She's the perfect little elf as she hands Nate and Trish each a cigar, her smile widening when she gets to me.

There are two left in her hand, and I'm impressed.

Not just because my wife is not usually fond of joining in on my smoking habit, but because I have no doubts that she's "prepared" each of them the way I asked.

I choose one and copy Nate, bringing it in for a sniff. It's woody and sweet and Sabrina all wrapped up in one scent, and fuck if it isn't the most glorious thing I've ever put to my nose.

"Cohibe Behikes," he says. "Excellent taste."

He has no idea.

I'd prefer to drag Sabrina off to a dark corner at this point, but I'd never dream of offering a cigar without offering to smoke. And I'm particularly eager to smoke this particular puro myself.

I'm equally eager to see Sabrina put a stick between her lips, so I make the only suggestion that makes sense: "To the balcony, then?"

FOUR

IT'S COLD OUTSIDE, which isn't a surprise on a December night in New York City, not that I can feel it with the Santa suit still on. I'd be concerned about Sabrina dressed in her skimpy outfit if she hadn't requested high-power heaters to be set out.

That party planning detail was specifically because she knew I'd want to come out here at some point for just this reason. *See, Nate? She does take care of me.*

Of course, I only knew she'd prepared it because I'd been told when I went to put in the request myself and discovered she'd already done it.

Not the point.

Nate, thankfully, has a lighter in his pocket and a straight cutter on his keychain, which means I don't have to fumble with my costume to find mine. Soon enough, the ends are trimmed and lit, and I take my first puff and sigh.

"It's really good," Trish says while I'm still savoring the first draw.

"Best cigar I've ever tasted." I'm aware that it sounds self-complimentary, but I only care that Sabrina hears it.

Even in the poor light of the heaters, I can tell her cheeks pink.

Nate's a fellow connoisseur, and it takes a moment to assess the flavor. "It's rustic and dry and do I detect a floral note?"

"Definitely a floral note," I say, eyes pinned on Sabrina. It's all I can do not to lick my lips, the taste of her is so powerful that I don't even mind that it's tainted the purity of the Cuban.

I'm aroused, of course. But I tend to live my life with a constant semi since Sabrina's been around, so I'm used to the mild discomfort of being turned on. Knowing she's also aroused, that she's on the edge with anticipation, makes it all the more bearable.

Until she pulls her cigar from her mouth and sweeps her tongue around her lips. Then she says, "I'm not usually a fan of cigars, and even I like this one."

...and my cock officially decides it's time to whittle this party down to two and move it elsewhere. "That's it. I'm going upstairs to change out of this costume." I put out my cigar first, then take Sabrina's from her and put it out as well, which causes her to gape in surprise.

"I was enjoying that," she exclaims.

"No, you weren't. You were enjoying how much I was enjoying it." I manage to locate my tux pocket inside the Santa suit and stuff the cigars inside. "In case you aren't here when we return," *if* we return, "Trish, Nate, always a pleasure. Sabrina, let's go."

After somehow being persuaded to take Nate's camera to his office for him—why he brought his own down when there was a hired photographer is beyond me; that's artist's for you—I grab Sabrina by her elbow and direct her inside and through the ballroom.

She quibbles with me the entire time about whether her leaving with me counts as a demand or not:

"Doesn't count if it's not dirty," I remind her.

"It's going to get dirty soon enough."

"You don't know that."

"Yeah, right I don't."

"Not to mention that if it were a demand, you would have to actually do the thing I asked, which from my standpoint, you haven't, since I'm dragging you along."

"You're only dragging me because you're too impatient to let me walk at my own speed. It's seven. It counts."

By the time we reach the elevator, I'm done with the argument. Once the doors close and I've pushed the button to our floor, I slam her against the back wall and pin her there with my hand on her throat. "It doesn't matter if you do or don't cross off number seven. With or without it, you aren't any safer from what's to come."

She swallows and her pulse picks up, and even though I've given into her, I consider it a win. The whole point of the demand setup is that she enjoys being forced to do naughty things. The hand I have pressed against her windpipe is a reminder to us both that I don't need words for that.

Now that I have her attention, I let my gaze drift down to her mouth. I trace her bottom lip with my thumb. "Could you taste yourself like I could? When you puffed on that stick, did you enjoy the flavor of your cunt?"

She nods as well as she can with my hand keeping her in place.

"Please say you didn't go to the ladies' room to get them wet."

A smile appears as she shakes her head no.

"Tell me what you did."

"The attendant recognized me so he let me in without question. He kept chatting with me while I looked for the cigars, but as soon as I found them, a couple came to the window with their coat tickets. While they were talking, I turned my back to him, lifted my skirt, and put both cigars inside me at once."

My hand wanders lower as she talks, sneaking inside her dress to play with her nipple, and when she reaches the end of her story, I have to fight back a groan. "Santa's going to have to put you on the bad list, I'm afraid, Sabrina. Because that was so very, very bad."

"Does that mean I won't be getting anything for Christmas?"

"Not a chance." I'm ready to give her a thick steel rod right then and there.

Except then the elevator dings, and the doors open on our floor. "Telling me what happened in the coat-room—*that* counts as seven," I say, then release my hand from her neck. "After you, my dear."

She pouts in my direction for a full beat before she moves to leave. I follow behind, grinning at her frustration.

It's not that it's not real—I'm sure it is. I'm sure that she's pissed that I'm the one who gets to decide what counts as a demand and what doesn't. Pissed that I've taken her from her party before it's ended. Pissed that I didn't push the emergency button fuck her in the elevator.

But I also know that people can be wired to be many contradictory things at once. Sabrina's wired to get pleasure from being pissed. Or scared. Or degraded. Her fury right now is her favorite form of foreplay, and what she needs will follow soon enough.

She's only two steps down the hallway when she stops. "Where are we going?"

I'd planned to send her to my office, but the camera sling on my shoulder gives me an idea. "Nate's office."

My master will unlock his door, but I'm glad when I see he's left it open, and I don't have to dig around for my keys. Sabrina walks past the threshold and leans a shoulder against the wall, seemingly waiting for me to return the camera and then usher her elsewhere.

Instead, I turn on a lamp to illuminate the dark room without having the brightness of the overheads, and gesture toward the desk. "Hop up, helper."

I haven't forgotten I'm still in my costume. There's nothing sexy about the Santa situation, and I'm burning up inside the stifling fabric, but I have one more demand before it can come off. "Keep the dress on, but get your tits out where I can see them."

"Is this eight?" she asks coyly, as though she wants to agree upon the terms this time before following through.

"It's eight if you do it before I come over there and do it for you."

She doesn't hesitate after that, pulling both the dress and her bra down to expose her breasts. The cinched material acts like a bustier, pushing her tits up and out in an obscene display. Her nipples are sharp and pimpled and practically begging to be sucked, and it takes me a second or two before I remember what I want to do next.

"Thighs spread, skirt up." When she obeys, I lift Nate's camera and center her on the display, and fuck. She's a goddess. A portrait of filth and lust. Her hooded eyes, her wet mouth, her glistening cunt...

I hadn't planned on taking a picture. I'd meant to just make her believe I was loading our Art Director's memory card with naughty images rather than actually doing it, but seeing her on the screen, I have to push the button.

She hears the click of the device, and her lids pop open. "Isn't that Nate's camera?"

"Yep." I turn the camera out of landscape format and click again.

"You're planning to delete them after, right?"

She's both aroused by the prospect and mortified. This isn't the same as the time when I fucked her on Weston's desk in front of his security cameras. Then, the chance that he'd ever go back through the footage was slim. Of course, I sent him the tape to be sure he'd seen it, but that was neither here nor there.

What mattered was how scandalous it had felt while I was fucking her, and that had been just scandalous enough.

This was a great deal more scandalizing, because there was very little chance that Nate wouldn't look through his pictures of this evening at some point, and even if there were other pornographic images on his card—which would not be surprising—there was very little doubt that he'd see these.

I don't even consider easing her mind. "We're missing something." I'm not just attempting a redirect. The pièce de résistance has yet to be added. With the camera in one hand, I reach for a sharpie from Nate's desk organizer with the other. After uncapping the lid with my mouth, I bend down to write along the inside of Sabrina's thighs in big bold letters, traveling from left to right across her skin: **Santa's Dirty Filthy Slut**.

She glances down to read what I wrote, and her breath hitches. When she lifts her head again, I'm ready. The camera flashes as I click several times in succession, filling the screen with image after image of unadulterated erotica that makes my cock so hard, I can barely see straight.

Her voice is barely heard in the heavy fog of lust. "Donovan? The camera?"

Unable to hold back any longer, I toss the camera down on Nate's chair and tear off my hat/beard as I stride over to the desk. I wrap her long hair around my hand and pull her head back, forcing her lips to part as I do.

I lower my mouth until it's hovering an inch above hers. "The camera isn't any of your business, Sabrina. You made an earnest exchange—one favor at the price of ten demands" I know her cunt from memory, and she gasps when my finger lands directly on her clit. "If I demand you pose for me like a dirty, filthy whore, then you'd do best to oblige."

I maneuver my hand so that I can keep massaging her bud with my thumb while probing her with two fingers. "And even if you hadn't made that agreement, you do remember that you belong to me? That I decide who sees you and who doesn't."

"You said no one sees me but you." Her words come out uneven, and the next time I swipe my thumb across her clit, she jerks.

"Did I say that?" I remember plain as day that I did. I'd meant it. I still do. In fact, I swiped the memory card before I dropped the camera.

But she's so close, and I'm not going to kill her climax with the truth. Instead, I tease it out of her with my fingers and my empty threat. "Well, maybe I changed my mind."

Her body tenses, her muscles frozen as her orgasm crashes over her. Then a keening sound escapes from her lips. Her hips buck against my hand, and I cover her mouth with mine, desperate to swallow her cry. As though I can capture her pleasure inside of me and hold it there like it's mine because isn't it? Isn't every ounce of my happiness, my joy, my gratification sourced from her? There is nothing else I need. There is nothing else I want but this. The ability to give her *this*. The ability to love her like she deserves to be loved. To love her hard, and rough, and rich.

She's still cresting the wave of her climax when I

pull her to her feet. Her knees buckle, and I let her brace her hand on the desk instead of reaching for her so that I can finally get out of this damn sweaty wool garment. She seems to find her balance before I'm free so I issue my next demand. "Number nine: Put your tits against the window. Show the city how slutty you are for me."

Too cum-drunk to even think about arguing, she staggers over to the window and presses up against the glass, her skirt gathered at her waist and legs spread without me even asking, and damn if I wouldn't pay a million dollars to have a picture of her from the other side. We're several stories higher than the building across the street, though, so no such picture is possible, but it feels like she's on display for all of Manhattan, and I understand why that idea thrills her like it does. It lets her feel vulnerable and safe all at once. Lets her feel like she's being violated without the downside of actually being harmed.

That she trusts me to care for her like this...

As soon as I'm free of the Santa shit, I get my pants down far enough to let my cock out, and then I slam into her from behind. Fast and hard. One thorough strike that hits the end of her.

She cries out, but I don't stop to be sure it's a sound

of pleasure. With a hand braced on the window and the other wrapped around her so I can grip her breast, I pound into her with no regard to anything but the finish line. This is the place where I lose my focus. The only place. These are the moments when I struggle with control. When I'm buried inside of her, her cunt squeezing my cock like a vise, chasing my release like a hound that's hot on the tail of the fox. In these moments, my motives are singular and self-serving, and I drive after my pleasure with unyielding commitment. In these moments I only want to take. I want to defile. I want to use her and hurt her and love her too, but I want it to be messy and hard earned and unbridled and for me.

This is what she gives me.

This is what I'm owed.

This.

This.

This.

This.

This.

I'm back to my senses as soon as I've come. She's limp and out of breath, and I'm grateful she found release as well, but I'm also mad at myself. Ashamed. Not for how I've treated her because I know that she loves it. She'll consider the bruises I've left on her hips badges of honor. The guilt is because I didn't have control when I put them there. The shame is because I am not entirely without need. There are parts of me that are selfish and inconsiderate of others—inconsiderate of *her*—and like the monk who fails at keeping his eyes fixed on God, I consider this my sin.

I don't tell her this.

I've never told her this.

There isn't any point, and the confession of it would only draw more attention away from her and toward me. That's the last thing I want. I'm already weak.

I wrap my arms around her waist and kiss her neck, an attempt to recenter myself. She sinks into me and murmurs I-love-yous, and maybe that's what does it. Maybe it's how solid she is in my arms, how safe she makes me feel, or maybe it's Nate's words from earlier. Whatever the reason, my greed lingers, and I find myself considering other things I might want, other things I might take, other things she might give.

I don't think before I speak. "Have a baby with me," I say, my mouth near her ear.

It's the dirtiest demand of them all because it's all for me. We haven't talked much about children, really.

It hasn't come up. I haven't brought it up, mostly because I've been afraid I wouldn't be able to detach my wants from hers in the conversation, and while many couples might find that method of sharing dreams a healthy part of their relationship, it's not normally how we operate. Our modis operandi is she desires and I provide. As much as possible, I provide before she even has a chance to articulate the desire. I pride myself on knowing what she wants and needs, but this one thing—a baby—eludes me.

I don't know what she wants because I want it too badly for myself.

For better or worse, I've named that now, and there is no relief in the admission because now I'm alert, reading her cues, studying her reaction.

She tenses slightly, but it's brief. I've likely surprised her, and that's fair. With her next exhale, she's softer.

But then she pulls away.

Not entirely, just enough to turn around and face me. It's almost comical how serious she is, still in her Santa's helper outfit, her hair mussed, her tits hanging out.

"You want a baby?"

"Yes." My voice sounds raw, only barely not a squeak. I clear my throat. "Yes, I believe I do."

She nods, but she's not meeting my eyes. She's focused on her hand as it runs over my shirt, up the plane of my chest then back down. "I just...I'm still adjusting to the job," she says. "And Audrey's twins are due next month. I'm looking forward to being a really devoted aunt. Traveling back and forth to London to see her... I just don't think now's a good time."

As soon as I register the disappointment, I brush it off. "Of course. Right. Of course."

I straighten her clothing then attend to mine. I kiss her to let her know everything's good between us, to let her know I understand what she needs.

I *do* understand what she needs. Sometimes better than she does.

Nine dirty demands fulfilled instead of ten. She didn't say not ever. She said not now. I'll drop it for the time being. Let's just say she owes me one.

Sabrina owes Donovan...will he get what he wants? Find out in Kincaid.

Past and present weave together in Donovan's point of view for the next chapter in Donovan and Sabrina's life.

She was supposed to save me.

In a twist of fate, I rescued her. Since then, I've lived for her, breathed for her, overreached with my love.

She's still here, so I must be doing something right. But now I want more.

Except, a dangerous secret from my past threatens to come between us, forcing me to confront what kind of man I am.

And whether I'm the one who can save our future.

Kincaid *follows the Dirty Duet. It's not necessary to read all the books in the Dirty Universe before reading this, but it is recommended for a better reading experience.*

THE DIRTY UNIVERSE CONTINUES...

.

Meet all my Dirty Men.

Dirty Duet - Donovan Kincaid
Dirty Filthy Rich Men
Dirty Filthy Rich Love
Kincaid

Dirty Games Duet - Weston King
Dirty Sexy Player
Dirty Sexy Games

Dirty Filthy Fix - Nate Sinclair

Dirty Sweet Duet - Dylan Locke

Sweet Liar

Sweet Fate

Dirty Wild Trilogy - Cade Warren

Wild Rebel

Wild War

Wild Heart

Visit my www.laurelinpaige.com for content warnings and a more detailed reading order.

The Dirty Universe

Dirty Duet (Donovan Kincaid)

Dirty Filthy Rich Men | Dirty Filthy Rich Love

Kincaid

Dirty Games Duet (Weston King)

Dirty Sexy Player| Dirty Sexy Games

Dirty Sweet Duet (Dylan Locke)

Sweet Liar | Sweet Fate

(Nate Sinclair) Dirty Filthy Fix (a spinoff novella)

Dirty Wild Trilogy (Cade Warren)

Wild Rebel | Wild War | Wild Heart

Man in Charge Duet

Man in Charge

Man in Love

Man for Me (a spinoff novella)

The Fixed Universe

Fixed Series (Hudson & Alayna)

Fixed on You | Found in You | Forever with You | Hudson | Fixed Forever

Found Duet (Gwen & JC) Free Me | Find Me

(Chandler & Genevieve) Chandler (a spinoff novella)

(Norma & Boyd) Falling Under You (a spinoff novella)

(Nate & Trish) Dirty Filthy Fix (a spinoff novella)

Slay Series (Celia & Edward)

Rivalry | Ruin | Revenge | Rising

(Gwen & JC) The Open Door (a spinoff novella)

(Camilla & Hendrix) Slash (a spinoff novella)

First and Last

First Touch | Last Kiss

Hollywood Standalones

One More Time

Close

Sex Symbol

Star Struck

Dating Season

Spring Fling | Summer Rebound | Fall Hard

Winter Bloom | Spring Fever | Summer Lovin

Also written with Kayti McGee under the name Laurelin McGee

Miss Match | Love Struck | MisTaken | Holiday for Hire

Written with Sierra Simone

Porn Star | Hot Cop

PAIGE PRESS

Paige Press isn't just Laurelin Paige anymore...

Laurelin Paige has expanded her publishing company to bring readers even more hot romances.

Sign up for our newsletter to get the latest news about our releases and receive a free book from one of our amazing authors:

Stella Gray
CD Reiss
Jenna Scott
Raven Jayne

JD Hawkins

Poppy Dunne

Lia Hunt

Sadie Black

ABOUT LAURELIN PAIGE

With millions of books sold, Laurelin Paige is the NY Times, Wall Street Journal, and USA Today Best-selling Author of the Fixed Trilogy. She's a sucker for a good romance and gets giddy anytime there's kissing, much to the embarrassment of her three daughters. Her husband doesn't seem to complain, however. When she isn't reading or writing sexy stories, she's probably singing, watching shows like Billions and Peaky Blinders or dreaming of Michael Fassbender. She's also a proud member of Mensa International though she doesn't do anything with the organization except use it as material for her bio.

www.laurelinpaige.com
laurelinpaigeauthor@gmail.com